THE TECH BEHIND CONCEPT CARS

by Matt Chandler

CAPSTONE PRESS
a capstone imprint

Edge Books are published by Capstone Press,
1710 Roe Crest Drive, North Mankato, Minnesota 56003
www.capstonepub.com

Library of Congress Cataloging-in-Publication Data
Names: Chandler, Matt, author.
Title: The tech behind concept cars / by Matt Chandler.
Description: First edition. | North Mankato, Minnesota : Capstone Press, [2020] | Series: Edge books. Tech on wheels
Identifiers: LCCN 2019010896|
ISBN 9781543573046 (hardcover) | ISBN 9781543573084 (ebook pdf)
Subjects: LCSH: Experimental automobiles—Juvenile literature. | Automobiles—Technological innovations—Juvenile literature.
Classification: LCC TL147 .C445 2020 | DDC 629.222—dc23
LC record available at https://lccn.loc.gov/2019010896

Editorial Credits
Carrie Braulick Sheely, editor; Jennifer Bergstrom, designer; Eric Gohl, media researcher; Katy LaVigne, production specialist

Photo Credits
Alamy: dpa picture alliance, 19; Newscom: Abaca/Loona, 10, agefotostock/Jim West, 24, Cover Images/Volvo, 27, picture-alliance/dpa/Hauke-Christian Dittrich, 11, picture-alliance/dpa/Sven Hoppe, 8, picture-alliance/dpa/Uli Deck, 16, Polaris, 29, Polaris/Sam Simmonds, 14, Reuters/Lucy Nicholson, 23, Reuters/TT News Agency, 26, Sipa USA/Stephen Smith, 20, UPI/Keizo Mori, 18; Shutterstock: Chesky, 17, Mike Dotta, 28, Mikhail Bakunovich, cover, Nikita Anokhin, 13, Steve Lagreca, 4, 25, VanderWolf Images, 22, Zoran Karapancev, 12; SuperStock: Transtock, 6

Design Elements: Shutterstock

All internet sites appearing in back matter were available and accurate when this book was sent to press.

Printed in and bound in the USA.
PA70

TABLE OF CONTENTS

The angled headlights and gullwing doors help give the GAC Enverge a futuristic look.

CHAPTER 1

SHOWING OFF NEW IDEAS

When the doors opened for the 2018 North American International Auto Show, thousands of car lovers rushed in. They wanted to see the hundreds of cool new cars automakers had brought to the show. A sleek, silver vehicle really stood out. This car was the GAC Enverge.

The Enverge is an electric vehicle loaded with the latest technology. It's common for electric cars to be powered by two motors. The Enverge has four electric motors to boost power. Chinese automaker GAC put creativity into the vehicle's body design too. It has gullwing doors that open vertically. The doors can open with voice commands. A roof pod even holds a Segway scooter.

Like many other concept cars, the Enverge may never be fully produced for people to buy. But it showcases some amazing technology possibilities for the future.

FACT

The Batmobile began as a concept car. It was called the Lincoln Futura. George Barris bought the car. He transformed it into Batman's legendary ride.

What is a concept car? If you ask different people, you will likely get different answers. There isn't an official answer. But all concept cars are meant to show off new ideas or new technology. Most concept cars are not fully operational. Manufacturers sometimes use them to develop production models.

The Y-Job had a more streamlined look than cars of its time. The fenders wrapped around the car's front.

History of Concept Cars

In the early 1900s, cars became common on American streets. By the late 1920s, car companies were looking for ways to set their cars apart from the competition. The Lincoln LeBaron Aero Phaeton and the Auburn Cabin Speedster were two new designs that got a lot of attention. But most people consider the 1938 Buick Y-Job the world's first concept car. The Y-Job was a convertible. Electricity supplied power to lower and raise the top. The Y-Job introduced the technology of electric windows. Its headlights were hidden behind panels. Its door handles were even with the car body instead of sticking out. The Y-Job never went into production. But some of its technology became part of future Buicks.

convertible—a car with a top that can be put down

production—describes a vehicle produced for mass-market sale

The Vision Next 100 sits low to the ground and has a streamlined design to help it cut through the air.

CHAPTER 2

CONCEPT CAR BODY TECH

The first thing you notice about a car is how it looks. You can't see the engine or even the interior. You see the body. That's why automakers spend a lot of time and money creating attractive body designs. Concept cars often take body designs to the next level.

In 2016, BMW introduced its Vision Next 100 concept car. The car is loaded with amazing technology, but the body design got the most attention. BMW describes the car as its first "shape-shifting" vehicle. The car is fitted with 800 moving triangles. When the triangles move, the Vision's body almost looks like the skin of a snake. The triangles also serve a practical purpose. They are designed to shift and rotate when there is a possible danger. When a driver is focused on the road ahead, it can be easy to miss an object coming from the side. The car has sensors and cameras to monitor its surroundings. If it senses an object, the car activates the triangles to catch the driver's eye as a warning signal.

sensor—a device that detects change, such as heat, light, sound, or motion

Forged Composites

Automakers sometimes want their concept car bodies to improve on existing technology. Carbon fiber is a very strong, lightweight material. Car makers sometimes use it to replace heavy steel parts. But it costs more than steel, so its use for car bodies has been limited. Car company Lamborghini came up with a way to save time making carbon fiber and lower the cost. Through this process, they make forged composite carbon fiber. The process allowed Lamborghini to craft the entire body of its 2010 Sesto Elemento concept car from carbon fiber. The company then began using its new tech in production cars. In 2017, it released the Huracán Performante. The car's carbon fiber parts include the bumpers and rear wing.

The carbon fiber parts in the Huracán Performante help reduce weight.

the passenger body on the Vision Urbanetic

Two Bodies

Designers of the Mercedes-Benz Vision Urbanetic concept car figured two bodies are better than one. The 2018 self-driving concept car comes with two bodies. The bodies can be switched depending on how the car is being used. Each fits over the top of a single platform. One is designed to carry up to 12 passengers. The second is designed to change the car into a cargo transport vehicle.

Executive Design Director Karim Habib presented the Prototype 9 at the 2018 Canadian International Auto Show.

Back to the Future

Sometimes automakers look to the past instead of the future when designing car bodies. Nissan released the Infiniti Prototype 9 in 2017, but it looks like it came straight from the 1940s.

Nissan modeled the car after old roadsters. A roadster was a small car that had wheels that stuck out from the body. Many roadsters had convertible tops that folded down.

3-D PRINTING TECH

From the outside, the Mini John Cooper Works GP concept car looks like a fun sports car. But some of its coolest tech is inside. Automaker BMW used a 3-D printer to create part of the car's door panels and part of the instrument panel. BMW also used 3-D knitting technology to create seat sections. BMW's use of 3-D technology sets it apart from other car makers. Today buyers of some Mini vehicles can order 3-D-printed parts such as trim pieces.

Workers at Nissan cut and shaped the Prototype 9's body entirely by hand. This included a grille that looked like it was built from sword blades.

grille—an opening, usually covered by grillwork, for allowing air to cool the engine of a car

The Genesis Essentia has doors that open vertically.

CHAPTER 3

CUTTING-EDGE COMPUTER SOFTWARE AND ELECTRONICS

A concept car's sleek body may grab your attention first. But don't forget about the tech that could be packed inside. Recent advances in computer software and electronics have led to some amazing car tech.

Biometrics

If the Genesis Essentia concept car makes it to production, owners may be able to worry less about their cars being stolen. The computer system uses biometric facial recognition to scan a driver's face. The doors will open only if the car recognizes the face.

Fiat Chrysler plans to produce its Portal minivan concept car. This car takes facial recognition a step further. It identifies a driver's face and stores this information in its computer. The system then matches each driver with his or her preferred seat position, lighting, radio stations, and other settings.

Some concept cars have eye recognition programs to identify drivers. The driver looks into the rearview mirror, and the computer takes a photo of his or her eyes. If there is a match, the driver can operate the car.

biometric—relating to the measurement and study of unique physical or behavioral characteristics

software—the programs used by a computer

Amazing Artificial Intelligence

What if your car had a computer that could think and learn like a human? What if it could make decisions for you? Designers continue to explore and test artificial intelligence (AI) in cars. They are especially focused on using it in cars with self-driving features. For fully self-driving cars to become a reality, AI needs to work smoothly.

the interior of the Concept-I

FROM CONCEPT TO PRODUCTION

Many common features in production vehicles began as ideas in concept cars. These include power windows, airbags, and cruise control. Today many cars offer parking assist. A car with this feature uses cameras and sensors to take over and park the car. Volkswagen created parking assist in 1992 and put it in the Futura concept car. But it required a large computer in the trunk, making the feature unfit for widespread use. Self-parking became a reality 11 years later when Toyota released the Prius.

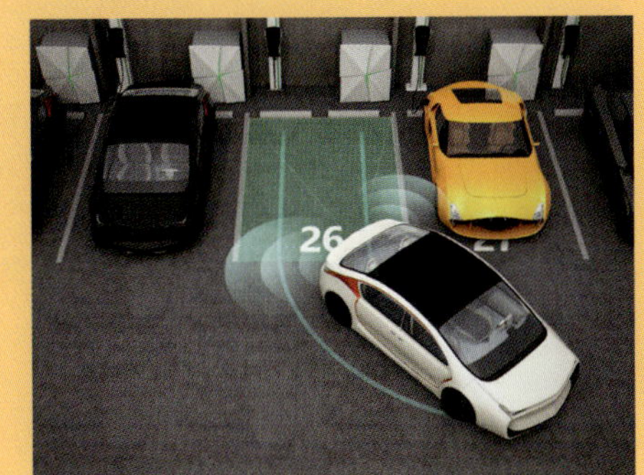

Toyota's Concept-I took AI to a new level. The concept car can sense the emotions of a driver. For example, the car might sense when a driver is feeling angry. An angry driver may drive faster or more recklessly. The car's AI then might offer the driver suggestions, such as to slow down. If the driver doesn't respond, the AI can take control of the vehicle for increased safety.

artificial intelligence—the ability of a machine to think like a person

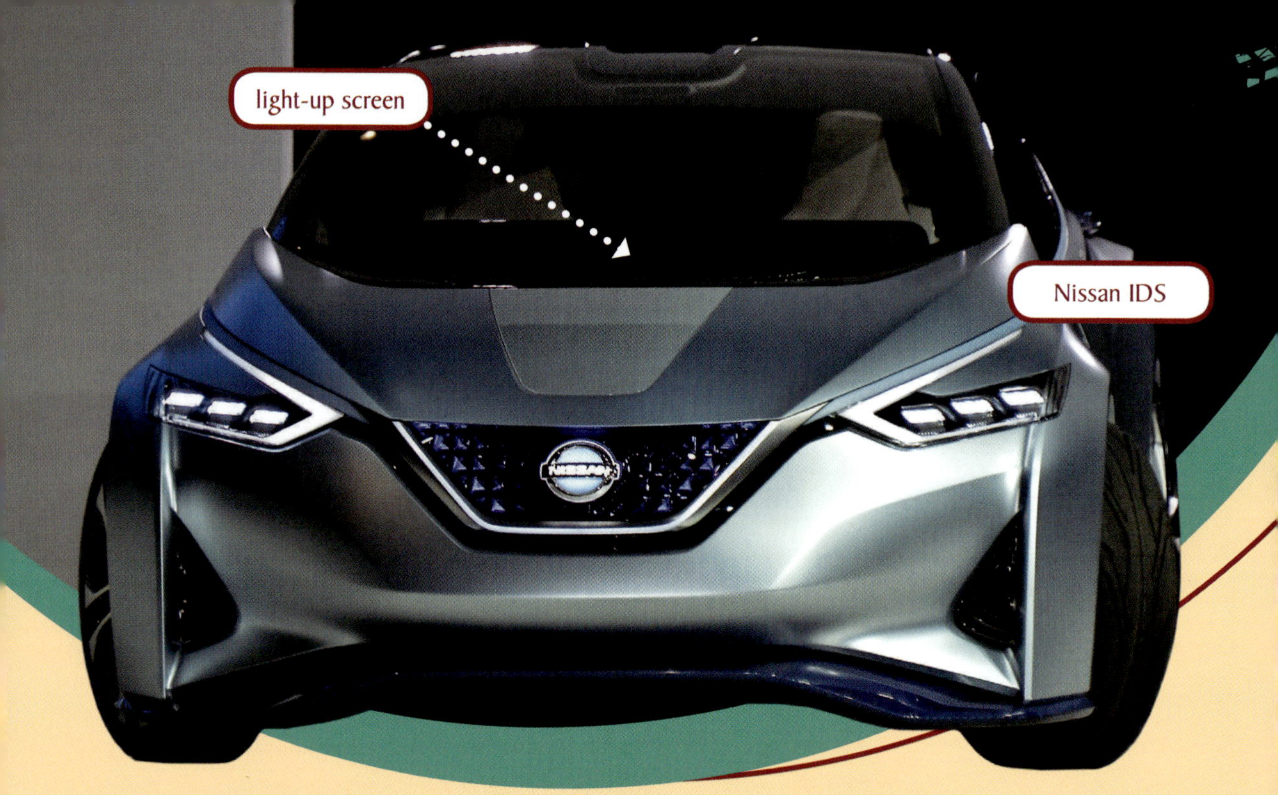

Awesome Electronics

Concept cars are loaded with electronics. Huge display screens light up in front of drivers. Cars that can switch between manual driving and self-driving mode often have two different display setups. Sometimes the steering wheel automatically tucks into the dash in self-driving mode. The Nissan IDS has a screen above the dash that can light up. The screen can display messages to other drivers or people walking nearby. The interiors of some cars have different lighting setups that drivers or passengers can change.

FACT

Some car makers are designing systems that can respond to a person's voice commands. They would allow drivers to change the music or lighting.

COMPUTER TESTING

Because many concept cars are designed without working engines, computer tests can be especially helpful for concept cars. For example, designers often use software to see how air would flow over the car. These tests help designers create aerodynamic cars.

Sometimes designers test their cars in wind tunnels after doing aerodynamic testing on computers.

acrodynamic—built to move easily through the air

manual—done by hand and not by machine

Volkswagen designed the Atlas Cross Sport to be stylish, but still useful for families.

CHAPTER 4

POWER CHOICES

Not every concept car comes with a solid plan for how it will be powered. But if a carmaker does have a plan, it usually includes ideas for how powertrain tech can move forward. The powertrain includes the engine, transmission, and axles that work together to get a car moving.

Many companies are designing concept cars with electric engines. These engines are more environmentally friendly than gas-powered engines. Some companies are finding ways to make electric car motors lighter and more efficient. Designers are experimenting with in-wheel electric motors. In this setup, a motor is attached to each wheel. It makes the car more efficient because the power has to travel less distance than in a standard setup.

Hybrid vehicles are another focus for car companies. These cars run on both gasoline and electric power. Volkswagen released the Atlas Cross Sport concept car in 2018. It offers drivers a new tech option called GTE mode. This mode makes the gas engine run as well as both of the car's electric motors. With all of the engines running, it can accelerate faster.

accelerate—to increase the speed of a moving object

efficient—not wasteful of time or energy

transmission—the series of gears that send power from the engine to the wheels

Harnessing More Horsepower

For some car enthusiasts, it's all about power. How fast can the car go? How quickly can it accelerate? Concept cars give these people the chance to imagine what power levels their dream cars might have someday.

A common way to increase power of gas-powered cars is by adding a turbocharger or supercharger. Both a turbocharger and a supercharger force more air into the engine. The air causes a more powerful explosion in the engine, creating more power. Some automakers use these systems in their hybrid concept cars.

Mercedes showed its AMG GT sedan at the 2017 International Motor Show in Frankfurt, Germany.

The Chaparral 2X Vision Gran Turismo was first presented at the Los Angeles Auto Show.

The 2017 Mercedes AMG GT sedan concept car came with two turbochargers for its gas engine. Its electric motor drove the rear wheels. Together the system was said to make 805 horsepower.

The 2014 Chevrolet Chaparral 2X Vision Gran Turismo was designed with a completely different power system in mind. A giant laser, batteries, and a generator would work together to create thrust. The system would help the car accelerate quickly.

FACT

Chevrolet designed the Gran Turismo as a way to celebrate the 15-year anniversary of the release of the popular video game *Gran Turismo*.

generator—a machine used to convert mechanical energy into electricity

horsepower—a unit used for measuring an engine's power

thrust—the force that pushes a vehicle forward

Alternative Power

As electric cars gain popularity, automakers are exploring the next environmentally friendly technology. Gas-powered cars produce carbon monoxide and other gases that pollute the air. Hydrogen cars produce only oxygen and water, so they don't harm the environment. But there is a lot of work to be done before hydrogen replaces gas as a primary fuel source.

FACT

The Toyota Mirai has a hydrogen tank that has three layers to keep it from being damaged. The tank is designed with carbon fiber.

a Toyota hydrogen tank designed for a concept car

One drawback of hydrogen is that it is very flammable. If a hydrogen fuel tank was damaged, it could cause a fire. The Chevrolet Colorado ZH2 is a concept vehicle with an idea to solve this problem. General Motors is working with the U.S. Army on the vehicle. They have created a hydrogen tank that is bulletproof. GM has also added tech that will immediately vent the hydrogen out of the top of the tank if it is damaged.

The Chevrolet Colorado ZH2 sits up high to help it travel on rough ground.

The light bar goes around the Volvo 360c to make it visible to people on all sides.

CHAPTER 5

THE FUTURE OF CONCEPT CARS

The future of concept cars is limited only by designers' ideas. From high-tech materials to creative body designs, concept cars are sure to get a lot of attention.

A horn on the 360c is designed to send sound directly to pedestrians.

Solutions for Self-Driving Cars

Companies including Waymo, Volvo, and Tesla have driven millions of test miles in fully self-driving cars. But there are still safety concerns and other issues companies need to solve before these cars are ready for customers to buy. Concept cars can offer possible solutions. For example, Volvo came up with an idea to help with communication between pedestrians and other road users. The Volvo 360c concept car comes with speakers that make different sounds. One sound is used for when the car will go. Another is used for when the car is slowing down or speeding up. The system also comes with a light bar that changes color and patterns based on what the car will do next. A system like this could increase safety if fully self-driving cars become a reality.

Different Types of Vehicles

Some car companies are focusing on developing different types of concepts besides cars. Bosch has developed a shuttle concept that would run in cities. British aerospace company Rolls-Royce is developing a concept for a personal flying vehicle. The vehicle's six propellers run on electric power, and it can carry five passengers. Aston Martin partnered with Rolls-Royce to design the Volante Vision concept. This flying vehicle offers a solution for traffic jams. It is designed with vertical takeoff ability to fly like a helicopter!

Airbus, Italdesign, and Audi worked on the Pop.Up Next concept. The small two-seat car can unhook from its frame, and a drone would carry it into the air. With this vehicle, traffic jams wouldn't be a problem!

The Tesla semitruck concept is made with carbon fiber and plastic to make it lightweight.

Tesla made an electric semitruck concept. Tesla expects the truck to travel up to 500 miles (805 km) on a single charge with a full load.

The possibilities of concept cars in the future are almost endless. Car enthusiasts go to shows such as the Geneva Motor Show and the North American International Auto Show to see what exciting new concept car designs will be there. If you were designing a concept car, what would you make?

GLOSSARY

accelerate (ak-SEL-uh-rayt)—to increase the speed of a moving object

aerodynamic (air-oh-dye-NA-mik)—built to move easily through the air

artificial intelligence (ar-ti-FISH-uhl in-TEL-uh-junss)—the ability of a machine to think like a person

biometric (by-oh-ME-trik)—relating to the measurement and study of unique physical or behavioral characteristics

convertible (kuhn-VUHR-tuh-buhl)—a car with a top that can be put down

efficient (uh-FI-shuhnt)—not wasteful of time or energy

generator (JEN-uh-ray-tur)—a machine used to convert mechanical energy into electricity

grille (GRIL)—an opening, usually covered by grillwork, for allowing air to cool the engine of a car

horsepower (HORSS-pou-ur)—a unit used for measuring an engine's power

manual (MAN-yoo-uhl)—done by hand and not by machine

production (pruh-DUHK-shuhn)—describes a vehicle produced for mass-market sale

sensor (SEN-sur)—a device that detects change, such as heat, light, sound, or motion

software (SAWFT-wair)—the programs used by a computer

thrust (THRUHST)—the force that pushes a vehicle forward

transmission (transs-MISH-uhn)—the series of gears that send power from the engine to the wheels

READ MORE

Bethea, Nikole Brooks. *High-Tech Highways and Super Skyways: The Next 100 Years of Transportation.* Our World: The Next 100 Years. North Mankato, MN: Capstone, 2017.

Enz, Tammy. *Artificial Intelligence at Home and on the Go: 4D An Augmented Reading Experience.* The World of Artificial Intelligence 4D. North Mankato, MN: Capstone, 2019.

Geddis, Norm. *Concept Cars: Past and Future.* World of Automobiles. Broomall, PA: Mason Crest Publishers, 2019.

INTERNET SITES

Motor1.com: Concept Cars
https://www.motor1.com/news/category/concept-car/?p=2

The 21 Greatest Concept Cars of All Time
https://www.msn.com/en-ca/autos/enthusiasts/the-21-greatest-concept-cars-of-all-time/ss-BBSBIfA

What Keeps Concept Cars from Making it to Market?
https://auto.howstuffworks.com/concept-cars-on-market.htm

INDEX